To Hugo

With love from

Isabella ♡

Johannesburg, South Africa

A BAOBAB IS BIG

& other verses from Africa

Written & Illustrated by Jacqui Taylor

For my Mum & Dad
With Love

Acknowledgements

Thanks firstly to Struik Lifestyle for affording me the opportunity to publish this, my second book with them.
My gratitude goes especially to Linda De Villiers for her unstinting enthusiasm and support,
also to Cecilia Barfield for her careful, and ever tactful, editing of my text.

To the six-year-olds at the Harare International School, especially little Lilith, who renewed
my passion to give joy through words and pictures.

To Patrick Mavros, whose remarkable silver sculpture of a baobab and accompanying story,
were the initial inspiration for this book.

To Ian Murphy, Troy Reid and James Keegans, for invaluable technical advice.

To the amazing network of friends and relatives who have encouraged and prodded me along.
To Laura for her steadfast friendship and excellent impromptu editing. To my children, Chris and Laurie, for their
forthright criticisms and observations, and thanks to Julian for the aeroplane anecdote!

Lastly, to Ash, for his constant love and unfailing humour throughout, even across the continents.

Struik Lifestyle
(an imprint of Random House Struik (Pty) Ltd)
Company Reg. No. 1966/003153/07
Wembley Square, Solan Road, Gardens, Cape Town 8001
PO Box 1144, Cape Town, 8000, South Africa

www.randomstruik.co.za

First published in 2004 by Struik Publishers
Reprinted in 2005, 2008, 2009, 2010, 2012, 2013

Publisher: Linda de Villiers
Editor: Cecilia Barfield
Design manager: Petal Palmer
Designer and illustrator: Jacqui Taylor
Reproduction: Hirt & Carter Cape (Pty) Ltd
Printing and binding: Times Offset (M) Sdn Bhd

ISBN 978-1-86872-946-3

Contents

A baobab is big,
It is a kind of tree.
It only grows in Africa,
It is much bigger than me.

It looks to me the baobab
Is growing upside down.
With top below ~ where roots should be ~
And roots up instead of crown.

They say a long, long time ago
That in an angry fit,
A god ripped up the baobab,
And then misplanted it!

Sometimes inside a baobab
You find a hollow space.
Good for a game of hide and seek,
Or just a quiet, private place.

The baobab is a grand hotel
To many animals I know.
A bushbaby, a big baboon,
A noisy hornbill, a gecko.

Sometimes a little rain collects
High in the branches of the tree,
Where creatures come to bath and drink
When it's as hot as hot can be.

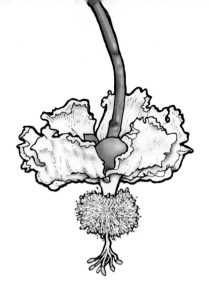

The baobab it has a flower
Of pure and creamy white,
A bloom that you must never pick ~
It's far too beautiful a sight.

The baobab it has a pod
With seeds inside I like to eat.
Their name is 'cream of tartar',
They are my favourite treat.

If I could have a baobab
All of my very own,
I'd choose the hugest, hollow one,
And call it 'Home Sweet Home'.

Hallo Aloe,
How are you?
Reaching up
To sky of blue.
It seems to me
Your claims to fame
Are leathery leaves
And flowers of flame.

Greetings Mr Tortoise
Inside your tortoise shell.
I'm sure that you feel safe in there,
But it's fine out here as well!

One day Lilith lay lazing
In the shade of a big tree.
She watched the clouds sail up above,
Like ships upon the sea.

The clouds all changing with the wind,
She saw them form and grow
Into a hundred different shapes,
From her shady spot below.

Lilith was peaceful lying there,
Lost in the shifting cloud.
When suddenly she heard a shout,
That was close and rude and loud!

The voice said 'Go away!'
And seemed to come from out the sky.
Poor startled Lilith ran inside
Where she began to cry.

'Oh Mum, I was just lying there,
Just dreaming peacefully,
When someone rude yelled
"Go away" from the top of the big tree.'

Her mother hugged her,
Then she said, 'My darling, what you heard,
Was not someone being rude or mean,
But that old grey loerie bird!'

'It is an early warning call
To tell his friends to run away,
From any other wild creatures
Who might eat his friends as prey!'

So they went out into the garden
To find the culprit in the tree.
And Lilith said, 'You naughty bird,
To play such a trick on me!'

The springbok is a small gazelle,
Who knows the art of pronking well.
If he ran our school hurdle race,
He'd beat us all and win first place!

Dad went on an aeroplane,
We went to say goodbye.
He climbed onto the jumbo jet,
It took off into the sky.

We watched the giant silver plane
Growing smaller by the minute.
I asked my Mum, 'The plane's so small,
How can Daddy still be in it?'

Marty found a monster mango,
The biggest one he'd ever seen!
It hung there ~ most magnificent,
Sadly for Marty ~ still quite green.

So Marty went out every day
To check if it was red.
He thought of how he'd eat it,
He dreamt of it in bed!

He'd save the monster mango
For a hot and sultry day,
Then run a cool refreshing bath
While his sister was at play.

He'd hang a sign upon the door
Saying, 'LEAVE ME (PLEASE) IN PEACE!'
Put on his swimming costume,
And climb in the bath to feast!

At last, when ripe and ready,
Marty picked the colossal treat.
And with it hidden in his shirt,
He beat a quick retreat.

Marty hid the marvellous mango
Under his bed inside a shoe,
And waited for a sultry day
To see his secret through.

And soon enough there came a day
That was very, very hot.
So sign displayed and cool bath run,
Marty carried out his plot.

But as he sank his hungry teeth
Into the juicy treat,
He heard the sound of voices
And fourteen little feet.

Then round the door came seven heads,
His sister's being one.
And in unison they chorused,
'Oh please, can we have some?'

What did he say, 'Please go away,'
Or, 'No, the mango's mine?'
Did he say, 'Shoo' or 'Scat' or 'Boo?'
Three cheers for Marty! Not this time ...

Instead he said, 'OK, I s'pose,
Because although there's only one,
It is so very, very big,
And sharing is more fun.'

Last night I had a funny dream
That I was very small.
I went walking in the garden,
Where the grass was very tall.

I came upon a giant snail,
And terrified, I ran to hide.
'Don't be afraid,' the snail said,
'Instead, come for a ride.'

So I climbed upon the snail's back,
And off we slithered at a pace,
To meet with other garden creatures,
Larger than life and face to face.

First I met a daddy-long-legs
Carrying some precious eggs.
So I guess this spindly spider,
Was in fact, a mum-long-legs!

Next we found a gang of aphids
Who were busy in the throes,
Of munching on a lovely lunch ~
That being ... Dad's best rose!

Then down and through the flower pots,
We found a gecko, pink and shy.
I marvelled at his lightning tongue,
When he caught a passing fly.

From there into the vegetables,
Where in amongst the carrot trees,
I met a giant earthworm,
Who was as pleasant as you please.

He said to me, in quiet tones,
'Now listen carefully,
For your dream has taught a lesson.
You have learned to really see.'

'That whether you are big or small
You have a right to be alive,
That spider, bee and tiny ant
All struggle to survive.

And recall, before you squash a bug,
Or swat a buzzing bee,
Remember then … when you were small,
You were afraid of *me*!'

Percy is my python,
A present from my pater.
He was quite small at first,
But he got much bigger later!

We got a perfect potjie pot,
And put a plump pillow inside.
My Percy coiled up in this bed ~
A picture of pure pride.

Percy grew and shed his skin,
As snakes will tend to do,
And sadly, Percy's potjie,
Was what he outgrew too!

My parents pitied Percy's plight,
So they went out and got,
A giant, king-sized, out-sized, huge …
ENORMOUS potjie pot!

percy's new potjie

So Percy has a new pot,
He's as pleased as pleased can be.
And his old potjie pot,
Is just the perfect size for me!

Kallie left her family
While on an African safari,
To join a little meerkat gang,
Out in the Kalahari.

She slept curled up in their burrow,
And basked with them in the sun.
She shared their meerkat cuddles,
And joined in their games and fun.

She took her turn at sentry duty,
Perched high on a termite's hill.
She babysat the kittens,
While the others ate their fill.

But Kallie was quite horrified,
When at her sandalled feet,
Was laid a giant scorpion ~
The most favourite meerkat treat!

'So sorry,' said our Kallie,
Listening to her rumbling tum.
'But I'd rather have an egg and chips,
And for that I need my Mum!'

The sun when it is sunset looks like a huge red ball,
And yet at midday, up above, it's bright and very small.

Fascinating Facts

The Baobab Tree

Botanical name: ADANSONIA DIGITATA Afrikaans name: KREMETARTBOOM
Shona name: MUUYU Ndebele name: UMKHOMO

The baobab is found in most countries south of the Sahara Desert ~ as far south as the Limpopo Province of South Africa, preferring hot areas with low rainfall. It is a huge deciduous tree that can grow up to 20 metres in height, while the trunk can reach a diameter of up to 12 metres. A baobab of this size may be well over 2,000 years old! Carbon dating of a tree in Zimbabwe, with a trunk diameter of 4.5 metres, proved the tree to be 1,010 years old.

The trunk itself can be tall and bottle shaped, or quite short and squat, while the crown is usually round and spreading. The bark of the baobab is smooth and silvery, tinged with a coppery colour. It folds itself into wonderful shapes that look almost like melting wax. Because the baobab stores water in its trunk, elephants will strip the bark and chew it for moisture. The bark can be used in the making of baskets, rope and mats. Water may be tapped from the roots of the tree and the young roots are sometimes cooked and eaten.

The leaves are dark green and hand shaped ~ they each have five leaflets that resemble fingers. In the winter season the tree loses its leaves. Many game animals eat the leaves of the baobab and cattle will eat the fallen leaves at the begining of winter. People cook the new leaves to make a dish similar to spinach.

At the start of the rainy season, new leaves appear and the tree produces single flowers that are approximately the same size as a soup plate in diameter! The blooms hang down from the branches like big, white, waxy bells. They are pollinated by bushbabies, bats, bluebottles (a kind of fly) and moths, who are attracted by their scent of carrion (decaying meat). The pollen can be used to make glue but picking a baobab flower is thought to bring bad luck. Fruit appears on the tree at the beginning of the dry winter season. The seed pods are 10~15 centimetres in length and are roughly oval in shape. Covering the hard pod shell is yellowish, velvety hair. Inside are brown, kidney-shaped seeds that are covered with a creamy-white, dry pith called 'cream of tartar', which contains lots of vitamin C and tartaric acid. This pith can be licked off or used to make a refreshing drink. The seeds can even be roasted, ground and used as a substitute for coffee or may be used to flavour soups and stews. Sometimes, a baobab will trap a small reservoir of water high in its branches. This well will be visited by many animals and birds during the dry season.

Many ancient baobabs develop hollows inside them that provide homes and shelter for all sorts of animals ~ including humans! One hollow baobab was turned into a small prison, one into a bus shelter, another into a bar and one into a lavatory ~ complete with flushing toilet!

All in all, the baobab is a magical, mystical, amazingly useful and unique tree.

The Bushbaby

There are several species of bushbaby found in southern Africa. Because they are so cute and cuddly looking, people sometimes keep them as pets. They are also known as night apes or 'nagapies'. Bushbabies are nocturnal and have huge eyes. They are covered in soft fur that is usually grey and have long tails. Their preferred habitat is woodland, where their diet of insects is plentiful. They will find a flat place high in the tree canopy to live, and sometimes even live in disused nests. The female produces two or three young, after a gestation period of four to five months. A family group will comprise between two and six individuals. If you hear a bushbaby calling at night, it is hard to imagine that such a cute-looking creature emits such a piercing shriek!

The Baboon

Baboons are mammals of the primate order. The only type of baboon found in southern Africa is the Chacma Baboon. An adult male can weigh up to 30 kilograms and grow to a length of 1.5 metres, an adult female baboon being slightly smaller. The female gives birth to a single offspring after a gestation period of six months. They have muzzles, much like dogs, and have large teeth. They are covered in coarse, yellowish-grey fur, with reddish-blue patches of bare skin on their rumps. Baboons are social animals, who live in troops with a strong family structure of up to 100 individuals. They live in many different habitats, apart from desert areas, and will eat almost anything, from fruit, roots, flowers and grasses, to slugs, insects, reptiles ~ even small mammals, such as young antelope! Farmers consider baboons a pest because they will take poultry and raid crops in the field.

The Hornbill

The hornbill illustrated in this book is the yellowbilled hornbill. There are 45 different species of hornbill found worldwide ~ nine of which are in southern Africa. Hornbills live in woodland and thornveld areas. They feed on fruit, insects and small reptiles, and often forage for food on open ground. Hornbills tend to be raucous birds. The largest hornbill found in Africa ~ the Ground Hornbill ~ has a deep, booming call that is sometimes mistaken for the roar of a lion! These birds are easily identified by their huge, curved bills and are all quite large birds ~ ranging from 40 to 90 centimetres in length.

The Gecko

Geckos are reptiles and members of the lizard family. There are hundreds of different types found all over the world, ranging in length from five to 16 centimetres. Most are nocturnal, making bark-like noises to communicate with one another in the dark. They have large eyes with pupils that reduce to the size of a pinprick in the day and enlarge hugely at night. Geckos have no eyelids, using their long, sticky tongues to clean and moisten the eye surface. Tongues are also used to catch insects. The tongue darts out quickly so that the prey sticks to it and is brought into the mouth. Geckos have adapted to many different environments and are found both in cold mountain areas and hot deserts. They are often found living in houses and are helpful to man by eating insects such as mosquitoes that can spread malaria. On their feet geckos have hairs and tiny claws, which allow them to climb walls or run effortlessly across ceilings. Female geckos lay one or two fair-sized eggs with hard shells from which the young hatch. The incubation period varies from one species to another.

The Aloe

Aloes are indigenous to Africa and to parts of the Middle East. They are succulent plants, of which there are more than 200 species. They are also evergreen plants, usually with sword-shaped leaves that have a serrated edge that is arranged in a rosette formation around a central stem. The flowers are tubular or bell-shaped, clustering on a long stem. Most aloes grow easily in warm, dry climates in rocky or well-drained soil. Some aloes are very small, while the largest aloe found in Africa ~ the tree aloe ~ can grow up to 15 metres in height. The sap taken from aloes is used for medicinal purposes as well as for a variety of cosmetic and beverage products.

The Tortoise

The correct scientific term for the shield reptiles ~ that is, tortoises, terrapins and turtles ~ is Chelonians. They are unmistakeable because they all possess an outer shell. The first fossils of these unique reptiles date back some 210 million years. In southern Africa there are at least 12 kinds of tortoise ~ the most common being the leopard tortoise. The shell is made up of a horny layer that covers a case of bone ~ the ribs, hips, shoulders and internal organs are all contained within this case. The weight of the shell causes the tortoise to be quite slow on its feet. Tortoises have a horny beak that looks a little like that of a parrot and they are herbivores (plant eaters). Their legs are covered with thick scales and they have clawed feet, while the head and tail are covered with leathery, scaly skin. If a tortoise is startled, it will pull its head, tail and feet into its geometrically patterned shell for protection. All tortoises lay eggs. The female digs a hole in the earth with her back legs in a warm, moist spot and lays her eggs inside it ~ where they are left to incubate. Incubation time can vary from four to 15 months and when the young hatch, they take care of themselves.

The Loerie Bird

The loerie illustrated in this book is the grey loerie or 'go-away' bird. It is large ~ about 50 centimetres in length ~ with a black beak and dark eyes. It has a crest on the top of its head and a long tail. Loeries eat fruit, and jump and spring along the tree branches ~ in between flying! The grey loerie is much plainer than its gorgeous, brightly coloured cousins. These are the purple-crested loerie, the Knysna loerie, Livingstone's loerie and Ross's loerie. The grey loerie is found from the west coast of Namibia, through northern Botswana, Zimbabwe, the Limpopo Province of South Africa, to the east coast of Mozambique. The grey loerie usually travels in groups of two to six. Its distinctive call of 'go away' is said to be used as a warning call of impending danger to other animals.

The Springbok

The springbok or springbuck is a member of the antelope family and is one of the national emblems of South Africa. Springbok are found mainly in the Northern Cape Province of South Africa, but also in Namibia, southern Angola and Botswana. They live on grassy plains or in dry scrub-land, eating grass, leaves, flowers, seeds and even digging for roots. The face and underside of the springbok are white, their backs are tan coloured and they have a reddish-brown stripe that runs the length of the body along the flanks. Both males and females have horns. A fully grown male stands about 75 centimetres high at the shoulder. The gestation period in the female is 24 to 25 weeks, after which time she gives birth to a single young. Springbok live in herds of ten to 200 individuals. Their most noticeable behaviour is that of pronking ~ leaping stiff-legged as high as three metres into the air ~ with head down and back arched. Pronking usually happens when there is a predator around, or if the springbok is uneasy or excited. During the mating season, the males will fight with one another, locking horns and wrestling ~ sometimes these fights result in terrible injuries or even death.

The Snail

The snail is a mollusc that reproduces by laying eggs. There are over 70,000 different types of snails and slugs worldwide. Snails have soft, slimy, greyish-brown bodies that can retreat back inside their hard, spiral shells if threatened. They have two sets of tentacles on the front of their heads; the eyes are situated on the rear set. On the snail's tongue ~ called a radula ~ are found as many as 150,000 small, file-like teeth, which help it to eat through plant matter at a rapid rate! Snails hibernate during the dry winter months and emerge in the rainy season. There are many species of snail in southern Africa, the most dangerous of which is a water-dwelling snail that carries the parasitic worm, which causes the disease bilharzia in humans. The snail illustrated in this book is the European garden snail, which, legend has it, was brought into Africa many years ago as an edible delicacy by a Frenchman living at the Cape during the Dutch occupation. Some escaped! Snails are generally considered pests and can cause a good deal of damage to gardens and crops with their voracious appetites.

The Daddy-Long-Legs

This spider is found widely throughout southern Africa. It is a fragile-looking creature, with a short, cylindrical body of about ten millimetres in length. The legs are very long and spindly ~ as much as four times longer than the body. Their webs are found in caves or dark, undisturbed places and are often found in homes and buildings. The web itself is not regular in appearance, but rather a mass of rather untidy strands. In the centre of the web, the daddy-long-legs will be found, hanging upside down. If disturbed, the spider will vibrate rapidly, becoming a blur and trying its hardest to be invisible! If removed from its web, the spider will move along with a peculiar bouncy walk. Some people think that it is a highly venomous spider; this is untrue ~ it is harmless to man. This falsehood may have arisen from the fact that the daddy-long-legs looks similar to the violin spider, which is poisonous. The female daddy-long-legs binds her egg sacs together with a few strands of silk and then carries them in her jaws. When the baby spiders hatch, they all perch on her head! These spiders should never be killed if found in the home, as they eat ants and other insect pests.

The Aphid

Aphids are generally considered to be pests by gardeners and farmers alike. They are also known as green fly, black fly or plant lice. They are small ~ about two to three millimetres long ~ and soft bodied. They cluster in large numbers at the tips or tender shoots of plants, feeding on the sap of the plant. Aphids are particularly fond of roses! Lady birds prey on aphids and ants 'milk' aphids for the special liquid honey dew that they excrete.

The Earthworm

The earthworm is common the world over and can grow up to a length of 30 centimetres. It has a segmented body, made up of as many as 200 cylindrical sections. Surrounding each segment are tiny hairs called setae (pronounced see-tee). These hairs help the earthworm to grip and wriggle its way through the soil. As the worm moves through the soil, it eats decaying vegetation and minute animals. It loosens the soil through all its burrowing, thereby allowing air and water to enter the soil. The droppings from the earthworm also fertilise the soil.

The Python

Pythons are non-venomous snakes that constrict or strangle their prey and then swallow it whole. A protected species, they are found in Africa, South America, southern Asia and Australia. The African rock python, or python sebae, illustrated in this book is Africa's largest snake and can grow to a length of six metres! It has a large triangular head, with a dark, spearhead-shaped mark on the top. The scales on top of the body form beautiful geometric patterns of greyish-green and brown. Underneath it is a pale creamy colour with dark speckles. Rock pythons prefer open savannah, rocky areas and places near water. Their prey consists largely of small mammals such as buck, monkeys and rats, but they also eat birds, fish and reptiles, including the occasional crocodile! Dusk or shortly after dark is their preferred hunting time. The female lays between 30 and 100 eggs in a disused burrow or cave and then coils herself around the eggs to incubate them. Each egg weighs about 150 grams and is the size of an orange. Eggs hatch in 65 to 80 days. Pythons, as all snakes, slough, or shed, their skins periodically as they grow. They make good pets as they are not aggressive snakes, but can inflict a painful bite (they have teeth!) if mishandled. Their suitability as pets is also limited by the fact that they grow so large.

The Meerkat

The meerkat is a small, endearing African mammal found in the drier areas of southern Africa, such as the Kalahari. Slight in build, it has a brownish-grey furry body with sharp, alert features. An adult meerkat stands no taller than 30 centimetres. Meerkats use their tails as a third leg whilst standing ~ in their most familiar posture ~ on their hind legs. They are social creatures and live in communal burrows in groups of five to 30 individuals. During the day they forage for food and eat termites, beetle grubs, small snakes, geckos, lizards and their favourite ~ scorpions. Whilst the clan is seeking out food, one meerkat acts as a sentry; only nursing mothers or babysitters are exempt. Perching itself high in the branches of a tree or on a termite mound, the sentry watches for predators with extreme vigilance. If one is sighted, the sentry gives a string of rapid alarm calls, at which all the meerkats make for the nearest burrow. Predators include lions, jackals, hyenas, cobras and birds of prey. Meerkats are affectionate ~ hugging, kissing and grooming each other liberally, all the while 'talking' to one another in a range of chatters, whines, grunts, growls and barks. If a member of the group is hurt, the others will nurse, groom and feed him until he is fully recovered. We could learn a lot about living in community by observing the meerkats.

The Scorpion

There are as many as 1,200 kinds of scorpion found in tropical or sub-tropical regions throughout the world ~ many of them in southern Africa. They belong to the same family as spiders ~ the arachnids ~ all of which have eight legs. Scorpions have a hard segmented body, large nippers and a long tail with a sting at the end of it. They live under rocks, bark or leaf litter. Most scorpions are nocturnal and all are predatory and carnivorous (meat eaters), feeding mainly on spiders and insects. One of the largest scorpions in the world, the rock scorpion, can grow to a length of 21 centimetres. All scorpions produce venom that will cause pain if one is stung, and a few have venom so toxic that it can kill small children or elderly people. (The meerkat appears to be partially, if not fully, immune to scorpion venom.) The scorpion is unusual in that it gives birth to live young, instead of first laying eggs. When the young are born, they climb onto the mother's back, where they remain until they shed their skins for the first time. Thereafter, they will leave the mother to fend for themselves.

The Sun

The sun is a star ~ a huge ball of burning gasses ~ that sustains all life on earth with its light and heat. The earth orbits the sun, held by gravitational forces. The sun, the earth and the other planets in our solar system belong to a galaxy called the Milky Way System. The Milky Way is one of 14 galaxies in the cluster to which ours belongs. In the Milky Way System alone there are over 100 million stars! The sun is the closest to us ~ almost 150 million kilometres away from the earth and its light takes eight minutes to reach the earth. The temperature at the sun's surface is around 5,500 °C, while the temperature at the sun's core is an astonishing 15 million °C!

Published works used for reference with grateful thanks

Newman's Birds of Southern Africa ~ Kenneth Newman ~ Southern Book Publishers
Southern African Birds ~ Ian Sinclair & Ian Davidson ~ Struik Publishers
Field Guide to the Trees of Southern Africa ~ B & P Van Wyk ~ Struik Publishers
Making the Most of Indigenous Trees ~ Fanie & Julye-Ann Venter ~ BRIZA
Trees of Central Africa ~ OH, K, D & P Coates Palgrave ~ National Publications Trust
Snakes and Other Reptiles of Southern Africa ~ Bill Branch ~ Struik Publishers
Reptiles of Southern Africa ~ Rod Patterson & Anthony Bannister ~ Struik Publishers
Snakes ~ Peter Stafford ~ The Natural History Museum Life Series
Tabex Encyclopaedia Zimbabwe ~ Quest Publications
The Bundu Book Series ~ Longmans
Meerkat Valley ~ Alain Degré & Sylvie Robert ~ Southern Book Publishers
Meerkats ~ Nigel Dennis & David Macdonald ~ New Holland Publishing
The Best of African Wildlife ~ Struik Publishers
Wildlife Southern Africa ~ Art Publishers

The End